JOHN WORSLEY

The illustrations by John Worsley in the *Award Adventure Classics* series, have greatly added to the impact and charm of these dramatic stories. Now well-established as a portrait painter and marine artist, John Worsley was in the navy during the war. Taken prisoner, he and a fellow officer constructed an astonishingly life-like dummy to help in their escape plan. After the war he was appointed adviser to the makers of the famous war film, *Albert RN*, which tells the true story of this remarkable feat.

ISBN 0 86163 066 1

Award Publications Limited 1982
Spring House, Spring Place
London NW5, England

© 1982 Victoria House Publishing

Printed in Belgium

Anna Sewell's

Black Beauty

Retold by Jane Carruth

AWARD PUBLICATIONS — LONDON

My
early
home

THE FIRST PLACE that I remember clearly was a large pleasant meadow with a pond of clear water in it. Some shady trees leaned over the pond, and rushes and water-lilies grew at one end. On one side of the meadow we could look over a gate at our master's house.

While I was very young I lived on my mother's milk, as I could not eat grass. In the daytime I ran by her side, and at night I lay down by the pond in the shade of the trees. There was a nice, warm shed in which we could shelter when it got very cold.

As soon as I was old enough to eat grass, my mother would go out to work in the daytime and return to the meadow in the evenings.

There were six other young colts in the meadow besides me. They were all older than I was, and some were nearly as big as grown-up horses. But we used to have such

fun together, galloping around the meadow, kicking up our heels in the air. Sometimes the play got rather rough, however, for they would often bite and kick as well as gallop.

One day my mother whinnied to me to come to her. Then she said, "The colts who live here with us are very nice, but you must remember they are cart-horse colts; they have not learned manners. You, on the other hand, have been well born and bred. Your father was well known and respected in these parts, and your grandfather won the cup for two years running at the Newmarket races. I know you have never seen me kick or bite anyone and I hope you will grow up gentle and good, never learning bad ways. Do your work willingly, always lift your feet up well, and never bite or kick, even in play."

I have never forgotten my mother's advice. I know she was a wise old horse, and our master thought a good deal of her. Her name was Duchess, but he often called her Pet.

Our master was a good, kind man. We were all fond of him and when my mother saw him at the gate she would whinny with joy and trot up to him. He would pat and stroke her, and say, "Well, old Pet, and how is your little Darkie?" I was a dull black so he called me Darkie. Then he would give me a piece of bread, and sometimes he had a carrot for my mother.

By the time I was about two years old I was beginning to grow quite good-looking. My coat had grown fine and sleek, and was bright black. I had one white foot, and a pretty white star on my forehead. I knew that people thought me very handsome, but my master would not sell me till I was at least four years old.

The next two years, however, passed very quickly and soon the day arrived when Squire Gordon came to look at me. He examined my eyes, my mouth, and my legs. He made me walk and trot and gallop, and he seemed to like me.

"When he has been well broken in, he will do very well for my needs," he told my master.

You may not know what breaking in is, so I will describe it. It means teaching a horse to wear a saddle and bridle and carry

a human being on his back. It means, too, that a horse must obey its rider and do as he asks quietly and willingly. Besides this, he must learn to wear a collar, a crupper and a breeching, and to stand still whilst they are put on; then to have a cart or a chaise fixed behind him, so that he cannot walk or trot without pulling it after him. A horse must learn always to do his master's will, even though he may be very tired or hungry, and he must not speak to other horses whilst he is being ridden or driven, nor must he bite or kick, nor really have any will of his own.

My master gave me some oats as usual before he began to break me in. Then after a good deal of coaxing he got the bit into my mouth, and the bridle buckled on. It was a nasty thing, but I knew my mother always wore one when she went out, and indeed all the horses did when they were grown up. So, what with the tasty oats, and my master's pats, kind words, and gentle ways, I began to get used to wearing my bit and bridle.

Next came the saddle, but that was not half so bad. My master put it on my back very gently, whilst Daniel, the kind old man who looked after all us horses, held my head. Then he made the girths fast under my body, patting and talking to me all the time.

I must say I felt rather proud when, one morning, my master got on my back and I carried him round the meadow on the soft grass.

Soon after that, my master took me to the smith's forge. There the blacksmith took my feet in his hand one after the other and cut away some of the hoof. It didn't hurt me, so I stood still until he had done them all. Then he took pieces of iron the shape of each of my feet and put them on, hammering some nails into my hooves so that each shoe was firmly held in place. My feet felt very stiff and heavy, but it didn't take me long to get used to them.

In time I got used to everything which had to do with being grown up, even the harness with the great sidepieces against my eyes, called blinkers, which meant I could not see to my left or right, but only straight in front of me when I was pulling the carriage.

My master often drove me in double harness with my mother because she was steady, and she taught me how to go better than a strange horse would have done. She said the better I behaved the better I would be treated, that it was wisest always to do my best to please my master.

"A horse never knows who may buy him, or who may drive him," she said. "It is all a matter of chance for us, so I say, do your best, wherever you are, and keep up your good name."

Birtwick Park

AT THIS TIME I would stand in the stable, and my coat was brushed every day till it shone like a rook's wing. It was early in May when a man came from Squire Gordon's, and took me away to the Hall.

My master said, "Goodbye, Darkie. Be a good horse, and always do your best." Unable to speak back to him, I nestled my nose into his hand, and he patted me kindly, before I left my first home.

Squire Gordon's Park skirted the village of Birtwick. We entered by a large iron

gate, where the first lodge stood, and then trotted along a smooth road between clumps of trees. We came to another lodge and another gate which finally brought us to the house and the gardens. Beyond this lay the home paddock, the old orchard, and the stables.

The first stall was a large square one, shut in at the back with a wooden gate. The others were common stalls, comfortable enough, but not nearly so large. The large one had a rack on the wall for hay and a low manger for corn: it was called a loose box, because the horse that was put into it was not tied up, but let loose to do as he liked.

The groom put me into this fine box. It was clean, sweet and airy, and I have never been in a better box than that. He gave me some tasty, fresh oats, patted and spoke to me kindly, and then went away.

When I had eaten my corn I looked round. In the next stall stood a fat little grey pony, with a thick mane and tail, a very pretty head, and a pert little face.

"How do you do," I said politely, "what is your name?"

"My name is Merrylegs," he answered. "I am very handsome, don't you think? I carry the young ladies of the house on my back. Are you going to live next door to me?"

"Yes," I said.

"Well, then," he replied, "I hope you are good-tempered. I don't like living next door to anyone who bites."

Just then a horse's head appeared over the wall from the stall beyond. It belonged to a tall chestnut mare, with a long handsome neck.

"So it's you who have turned me out of my box," she said, in a bad-tempered voice. "Do you realize you have turned a lady out of her own home?"

Of course I protested at this as it was merely where the groom had put me, and when, later on she went out, Merrylegs told me that her name was Ginger and she had a bad habit of biting and snapping. "It is her own fault that she was not allowed to stay in the box," he added.

The name of the coachman was John Manly and, after breakfast the next day, he came and fitted me with a bridle. He

did this so gently and spoke so kindly that I liked and trusted him at once.

On our way home, after a splendid gallop, we met the Squire and Mrs Gordon out walking.

"Well John, how does he go?" asked the Squire.

"First-rate, sir," answered John. "He is as fleet as a deer, and has a fine spirit too, but the slightest touch of the rein will guide him."

The Squire looked very pleased at this, and the very next day, he took me out

himself. I found he was a very good rider, and thoughtful for his horse too.

When we came home, the Squire's wife was waiting at the door.

"What shall we call him?" asked the Squire.

"How about Blackbird, like your uncle's old horse?" asked his wife.

"No, he is far handsomer than old Blackbird ever was," answered the Squire.

"Yes," she said, "he is really quite a beauty. What do you say to calling him Black Beauty?"

"Black Beauty — why, yes, I think that is a very good name. Yes, that shall be his name." And so that was what I was called.

Ginger

I WAS QUITE happy in my new home although I did miss my freedom and of course I missed my mother and my old master.

One day when Ginger and I were standing alone in our stalls she said, "If I had had your upbringing I might be as good-tempered as you, but now I don't believe I ever shall."

"Why not?" I asked.

"It's all been so different with me," she replied. "I never had anyone, horse or man, that was kind to me when I was young. I was taken from my mother as soon as I was weaned, and the man who looked after me and some other colts never spoke a single kind word to us. When we were out in the field, sometimes nasty boys would throw stones at us, and we came to believe that all boys were our enemies."

"I'm sorry," I said, "because it isn't true, you know."

"After I was broken in," Ginger went on, "I fell into the hands of a strong, brawny man called Samson, and he used to boast that he had never found a horse that could throw him. There was no gentleness in him, only hardness — a hard voice, a hard eye and a hard hand. He used to make me run round on a long rein in the training field till he had tired me out. And when he began to ride me, he would punish me with

his whip and spurs if I struggled against him."

I began to understand why Ginger was so bad-tempered when I heard this and I felt very sorry for her. But her story wasn't over.

"After I was broken-in," she began again, "I was bought by a dealer to match another chestnut horse, and then sold to a fashionable gentleman in London. My new master cared only to have a stylish turn-out. He made me wear a bearing rein which meant that my head was held in a high position for hours on end and I was not able to move it at all. I became very irritable and restless. I snapped and kicked when anyone came to harness me, and as a result I was soon sold."

"What a sad story," I said, feeling more and more sorry for Ginger. "What ever happened to you next?"

"My new master was just as hard and cruel as Samson had been. And one day when he had aggravated me more than usual I bit him. He began to hit me about the head with a riding whip. I hated him so much after that that I would go for him whenever he came into my stall. Soon he dared not enter it at all, and so it wasn't long before I was sold again . . ."

"And that time you came here," said I.

"Yes," said Ginger. "And I'm very happy. I really don't want to kick and bite; it's just that something comes over me as I remember the old days and I can't seem to help it."

"You must try," I said. "We are both fortunate to have such a good master."

One stormy day

THE LONGER I lived at Birtwick, the more proud and happy I felt at having such a home. Our master and mistress were respected and loved by all who knew them. They were good and kind to everybody and everything; people and animals alike.

One day, late in the autumn, the Squire told John he had to make a long journey on business. John decided to use the dogcart and to take me. There had been a great deal of rain in the night and now the wind was very high. It was blowing the leaves across the road in showers as I trotted along.

When we reached the toll-bar, and the low wooden bridge, John remarked that if the river was full, the water would be nearly up to the woodwork and planks, for the bridge was level and did not arch in the middle like most bridges.

The man at the gate said the river was rising all the time and he feared it would be a bad night. Hearing this, the Squire promised John that, when we reached the town, he would be as quick as he could

with his business. As it was, it was late in the afternoon when we started back. The wind was much higher now, and I heard the Squire say, "I have never been out in such a storm."

As we began driving through the woods, John remarked, "It would be very unpleasant, sir, if one of these branches came down on us."

The words were scarcely out of his mouth, when there was a groan and a terrifying cracking sound. Down came an oak, torn up by the roots. The great tree fell right across the road just in front of me, and only narrowly missed falling on top of us. I stopped instantly. John jumped out and was at my head in a moment.

"That was a very close thing," said the Squire, "what's to be done now?"

It was plain we could not hope to drive over the tree, so we had to turn back to go round by the longer road. But by the time we reached the bridge it was very nearly dark. We could just see that the water was over the middle of it, but as this sometimes happened when there was flooding, the Squire urged me on.

We were going along at a good pace, but the moment my feet touched the first part of the bridge I felt sure there was something wrong. I dared not go forward, and I made a dead stop in my tracks.

"Go on, Beauty," said the Squire, and he gave me a sharp cut then. I jumped, but I still dared not go forward.

"There's something wrong, sir," said John, and he sprang out of the dogcart and came to my head, looking across at the bridge. He tried to lead me forward. "Come on, Beauty," he said, "what's the matter?"

Of course I could not tell him, but I

knew very well that the bridge was not
safe.

Just then the man at the toll-gate on the
other side ran out of the house, waving a
torch about urgently.

"Hoy, hoy, halloo, stop!" he shouted.

"What's the matter?" the Squire
shouted back.

"The bridge is broken in the middle and
part of it is carried away. If you advance
you'll be into the river," shouted the toll-
gate man over the noise of the wind and
water.

"Thank God!" exclaimed the Squire,
amazed.

"You beauty!" said John, patting my

head. He took the bridle and gently turned me round to the right-hand road by the riverside.

The wind seemed to have quietened a little but it was becoming very dark. I trotted quietly along, the wheels hardly making a sound on the soft road. For a while neither Squire Gordon nor John spoke, and then the Squire began in a serious voice to say that if I had gone on, as they had wanted me to, most likely the bridge would have given way under us, and we would have fallen into the river. As the current was flowing very strongly, it was more than likely that we would all have been drowned then and there.

The mistress was waiting for us when we reached home. "I have been so anxious," she cried. "Are you really safe, my dear?"

"If your Black Beauty had not been wiser than we were, we should all have been carried down the river at the wooden bridge," the Squire told her.

I heard no more, as they went into the house, and John took me to the stable. Oh! what a good supper he gave me that night, a warm bran mash and some crushed beans with my oats. He gave me a thick bed of straw, too, and I was glad of it, for I was very, very tired.

The fire

SOME TIME after this, I heard James Howard, the stable boy, tell John that he was going to a new appointment. This made me quite sad for he had always been kind and thoughtful to all of us. I gathered that he was going to Clifford Hall as a groom and that Sir Clifford Williams was likely to be a very good employer.

It seemed the Squire had given James a very good reference, and that he was pleased that he should be taking up such a worthy position.

When all this affair was settled, James was asked by the Squire to drive him and the mistress to some friends some forty-six miles from our home.

Ginger and I were harnessed to the carriage.

James drove us so carefully and thoughtfully that even though we travelled thirty-two miles the first day, we were not tired. We stopped finally at the principal hotel, which was in the market place, and two ostlers came to take us into the stables.

After we had eaten our corn, a traveller's horse was brought in by the younger ostler, and whilst he was rubbing him down a young man with a pipe in his mouth wandered into the stable to gossip.

"I say, Towler," said the ostler, "just run up the ladder into the loft and get some hay for this horse's rack, will you? Only put down your pipe first."

"All right," said Towler, and went up through the trapdoor. Then James came in to look at us and give us a pat before retiring. Finally the door was locked.

I cannot say how long I slept, but I woke up feeling very uncomfortable. The air seemed all thick and made me choke. I heard Ginger coughing too, and one of the other horses moved about restlessly. It was quite dark and I could see nothing, but the stable was full of smoke.

I heard a low crackling and snapping in the hayloft and that noise made me tremble all over. By now the other horses

were awake, and some were pulling at their halters, others were stamping — all were becoming more agitated.

At last I heard steps outside, and the young ostler burst into the stable with a lantern, and began to untie the horses. But he was in such a hurry and so panicky himself that he frightened us even more and none of us would move. I looked upwards, through the bars of my empty rack, and saw a red light flickering on the wall. Then I heard a cry of "Fire!" outside, and the old ostler came in, quietly but quickly. He managed to persuade one horse to go outside, but the flames were now everywhere and the roaring overhead was dreadful.

The next thing I heard was James's voice, quiet and cheerful. "Come my beauties, it is time for us to be off, so come along," he said, with no trace of panic in his tone.

Then he came to me, tied a scarf lightly over my eyes, and patting and coaxing he led me out of the stable. Handing me over to someone standing nearby, he immediately rushed back into the burning stable and began bringing out the other horses.

The Squire came into the yard and I heard him calling to James. There was no answer at first and I heard a dreadful crash of something falling inside the stable. But the next moment I saw James with Ginger — and I was never so thankful!

"My brave lad!" said Master, patting James's shoulder. "Are you hurt?"

James shook his head, for he could not yet speak, so full was he with smoke and fumes, but some in the crowd echoed what the Squire had said. Just then there was a clattering and thundering over the stones and two horses dashed into the yard pulling the heavy fire engine behind them.

We got out as fast as we could into the open quiet market place; the stars were shining, and except for the noise behind us, all was still. The Squire led the way to a large hotel on the other side. There he left us with James, to return to his lady.

In the morning there was much talk of how the fire had started, but at last somebody said he had seen Dick Towler go into the stable with a pipe in his mouth, and that when he came out he had not got it. Towler denied that he had left his pipe behind, but no one believed him.

The rest of our journey was very easy and, a little after sunset, we reached the house of the Squire's friend. We stopped there for two or three days and then returned home.

I was glad to be in our own stable again, and John was equally glad to see us, and made a great fuss of us. Before he and James left us for the night, James said, "I wonder who is coming in my place?"

"It'll be little Joe Green who lives at the lodge," said John.

"Little Joe Green? Why, he's a child!"

"He is fourteen and a half," said John. "He is small but quick and willing, and kind-hearted too. I think he will do very well, and I have said I am quite willing to try him for six weeks."

The next day Joe came to the stables to learn all he could before James left. He learned to sweep the stable, and to bring in the straw and hay. Then he began to clean the harness, and help to wash the carriage. He was a nice, bright little fellow, and always whistled as he worked.

Merrylegs objected to being looked after by a boy, but towards the end of the second week, he told me confidentially that he thought the boy would turn out well, after all. Quite an admission for Merrylegs!

Ride for your life

ONE NIGHT, a few days after James had left, I had eaten my hay and was lying down in my straw fast asleep, when I was suddenly wakened by the stable bell which seemed to be ringing in my ear. I heard the door of John's house open, and his feet running up to the Hall. In no time at all, I heard him rush back and unlock the stable door. He ran inside, calling out, "Wake up, Beauty. You must go well now, if ever you did."

Almost before I could think, he had put the saddle on my back and the bridle on my head. He stopped briefly at his house for his coat, and then took me at a quick trot up to the Hall door. The Squire stood there with a lamp in his hand.

"Now, John," he said, "ride just as fast as you can! It is for your mistress's life, and there is not a moment to lose. Give this note to Doctor White. Rest Beauty at the inn, and be back as soon as you can."

grandfather who won the race at New-market could have gone faster.

When we reached the bridge, John would have let me go slower, but my spirit was up, and I was off again as fleet as before. At last we came to the town where all was deathly quiet except for the clatter of my feet. The church clock struck three as we drew up at Doctor White's door. John was off my back in a flash and ringing the bell and knocking at the door like thunder.

Dr White appeared and John wasted no time in telling his story. "I would come now," said Dr White, "but I have no horse."

"I would have liked Beauty to rest," said John, "but this is a matter of such urgency he will carry you till he drops. Take good care of him."

The doctor was heavier than John and not such a good rider. Still I did my very best, covering the distance home just as

John said, "Yes, sir," and was on my back in an instant. Away we went at the double, across the Park and through the village, and down the hill, till we came to the toll-gate. John called very loud and thumped urgently on the door. The man soon came out and flung open the gate. Seeing him preparing to close the gate behind us, John called out, "No! Keep your gate open, for the Doctor will be back immediately. Here's the money." And off we went again.

There was a long piece of level road by the riverside and John leant forward in the saddle and whispered low into my ear. "Now, Beauty, do your best." And so I did. I galloped as fast as I could lay my feet to the ground. I don't believe that my old

fast as I could. When we got home, I was nearly spent — my legs shook under me and I could only stand and pant. Joe rubbed my legs and my chest, but he did not put any warm cloth over my back, thinking I was so hot I would not like it. I grew more and more uncomfortable and oh, how I wished for John! But he was some eight miles away.

After a long while I heard John at the door. All I could do by then was to give a low moan, for I was in great pain. He was at my side in a moment, his hand on my neck, his face anxious. I could not tell him how I felt, but he seemed to know. He covered me with warm, thick rugs, and then ran back to the house for some hot water. He made me warm gruel, and

then I think I drifted into an uneasy sleep.

The next day I was ill; I could not draw breath without pain and so it continued for some time. John nursed me night and day, and the Squire often came to see me.

"My poor Beauty," he would say, "my good horse, you saved your mistress's life, Beauty! Yes, you saved her life."

I do not know how long I was ill, but the horse doctor came every day for some weeks. Poor little Joe Green was heart-broken, blaming himself. John for his part, could hardly be civil to him, but on the first day I could stand and take a few steps, John spoke more kindly to him. As I continued to grow stronger, John forgave him, and Joe became more cheerful and sure of himself.

The parting

I HAD SERVED Squire Gordon and his wife for three happy years when I heard that once again the lady of the house was ill.

John went about his work silent and sad, and Joe stopped whistling. There was a great deal of coming and going and Ginger and I had a lot of work to do.

Then one day I heard the sad news. The doctors had said that the mistress must leave England at once and go to a warm country for two or three years if she was ever to be well again. The news fell upon the household like the tolling of a death-bell. Everybody was sad and sorry.

Ginger and I were sold to an old friend of our master, the Earl of W—. for it was thought we should have a good home there. Merrylegs was given to the Vicar on condition that he should never be sold, and that when he was no longer able to work he was to be shot and buried. Joe was engaged by the Vicar to take care of him, and I could not help envying Merrylegs.

John had still to find a suitable household, but the Squire gave him the name and address of a gentleman in London who he thought would be able to help him find an appointment.

The sad day came at last when my master and mistress of the last three years left the Hall for ever. Ginger and I were harnessed up to take them to the station. John and Joe both came to see them off, and when the train puffed out of the station, Joe could not hold back his tears.

"We shall never see her again," John said, shaking his head with great sadness. Then he took the reins, mounted the box, and we drove slowly home. But it was not our home any more.

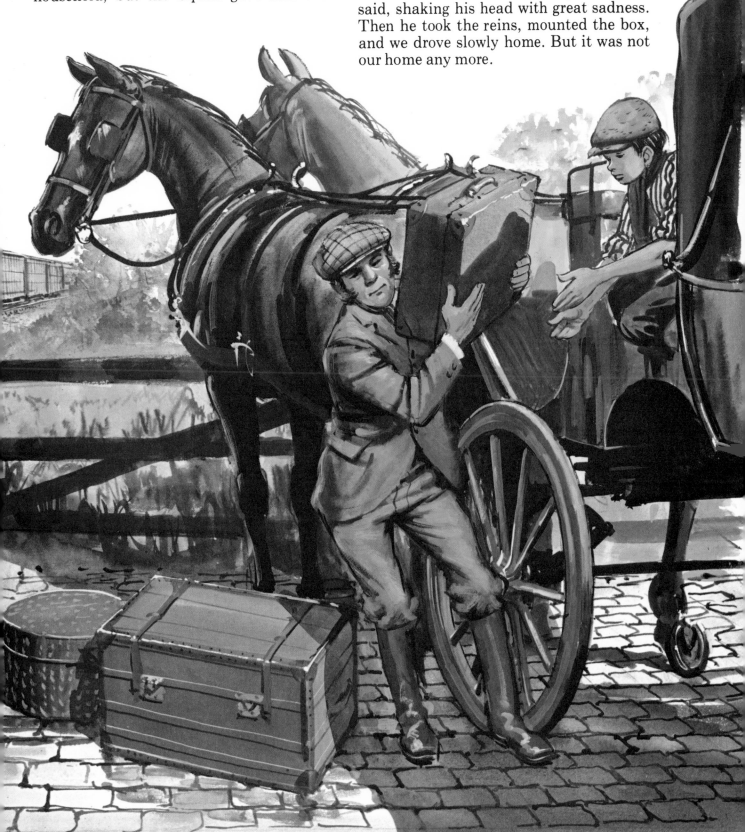

My new home

THE NEXT MORNING after breakfast Joe put Merrylegs into the mistress's low chaise to take him to the vicarage. Then John put the saddle on Ginger and the leading rein on me, and rode us across the country about fifteen miles to Earlshall Park, where the Earl of W—. lived.

We were taken to a light airy stable, and placed in boxes adjoining each other. In about half an hour John and Mr York, who was to be our new coachman, came in to see us.

John told him that we were among the best pair of horses to be found throughout the country, and York promised to look after us well. But just as they were going out of the stable, John stopped and said, "I had better mention that we have never used the bearing rein with either of them."

"Well," said York, "if they come here they must wear the bearing rein. His lordship is always reasonable about horses, but my lady — that's another thing! She insists on style. It must be tight up when my lady rides out."

"I am sorry, very sorry," said John, looking upset. "But I must go now or I shall miss my train."

Then he came to each of us in turn and his voice as he spoke softly to us, sounded very sad. I held my face close to him — it was all I could do to say goodbye. Then he was gone, and I have never seen him since.

In the afternoon we were harnessed and put in the carriage, and then led round to the front of the house, which was very grand. Two footmen stood ready, dressed in livery with scarlet breeches and white stockings. Presently we heard the rustling sound of silk as the lady of the house came down the flight of stone steps. She stepped round to look at us and I saw she was a tall, proud-looking woman with a haughty face.

"York," she said, "you must put those horses' heads higher, they are not fit to be seen."

That was the moment when I first learnt what it was like to wear a bearing rein. I

determined to make the best of it and do my duty, though it was now a constant trial instead of a pleasure to be taken out. Worse, however, was still to come.

One day my lady came down later than usual and the silk seemed to rustle more than ever. "Are you never going to get those horses' heads up, York?" she asked. "Raise them at once, and let us have no more of this nonsense."

York drew my head back and fixed the rein so tight that it was almost intolerable. But when he went to do the same to Ginger, she reared up so suddenly that York had his nose roughly hit, and his hat knocked off. Ginger was so upset that she kicked out wildly, catching me on the leg.

"Unbuckle the black horse! Run for the winch and unscrew the carriage pole," York shouted, holding his nose, "cut the trace, somebody, if you can't unhitch it."

One of the footmen ran for the winch, and another brought a knife from the house. Before long, Ginger was led away, a good deal knocked about and bruised. I stood there angry and miserable until York came and led me away, too.

Ginger was never again put into the carriage, but when she was well again, one of Lord W—'s younger sons said he would like to have her for hunting. As for me I suffered with that bearing rein for four long months as I drew Lady W—'s carriage.

Reuben Smith

I MUST NOW say a little about Reuben Smith, who was left in charge of the stables when York went to London. No one knew their business better than he did, and he was gentle and clever in his management of horses. I believe everybody liked him — certainly the horses did. But he had one great fault, and that was the love of drink. He used to keep steady for weeks — sometimes months — on end and then he would break out and be a disgrace to himself, a terror to his wife, and a great nuisance to all who had anything to do with him.

It was early in April, and the family were away until some time in May. There was a gentleman at the Hall by the name of Colonel Blantyre, and when he had to return to his regiment, Smith was told to drive him to town.

He chose me for the journey, and off we went. The journey to town was uneventful, but on the way back we left the carriage at the maker's, and Smith, who had taken a saddle with him in the brougham, rode me to the White Lion. Once there, he asked the ostler to feed me well and have me

ready for him at four o'clock. A nail in one of my front shoes had started to work loose on the way, but the ostler did not notice it till just about four o'clock. Smith did not come into the yard till five, and then he said he would not be leaving till six, as he had met some old friends. The ostler told him about the nail, but Smith said it would be all right till we got home.

He did not come for me at six, nor seven, nor, indeed, at eight. In fact, it was nearly nine before he came into the yard, and his voice was loud and rough.

Almost before he was out of the town he began to gallop, giving me sharp cuts with his whip, though I was going as fast as I could. The nail in my shoe worked right out, and my shoe became looser. As we neared the turnpike gate it came off altogether.

Smith was too drunk to notice anything. He spurred me on down the next long stretch of road over which no horse should have been ridden quickly as the surface was covered with large sharp stones. My shoeless foot was suffering dreadfully, but he urged me on with wild curses. The hoof was broken and split and the inside terribly cut by the sharpness of the stones.

No horse could keep his footing under such circumstances, what with the loose, uneven ground and the great pain. Finally, I stumbled, and fell with force on both my knees. Smith was flung off, and owing to

the speed I was going, he must have fallen with great force. I soon got to my feet and in the moonlight I saw that he lay motionless. I could do nothing for him except stand there and listen.

It must have been nearly midnight when I heard the sound of a horse's hooves. As the sound came nearer, I was almost sure I could recognize Ginger's step. A little nearer still, and I could tell she was in the dogcart. I neighed loudly, and was overjoyed to hear an answering neigh from Ginger, along with men's voices.

One of the men jumped out, and stooped down over the dark figure that lay on the ground. "It's Reuben Smith," he cried. "The horse must have thrown him. Now I fear he's dead."

The other man looked at my foot. "Look!" he suddenly said. "His foot is all cut to pieces, and so are his knees. Just think of Reuben riding a horse over these stones, with a hoof in that condition! Doubtless he was dead drunk."

One of the men led me slowly homeward, and I shall never forget that night walk, for the pain in my knees and foot was intense all the way.

Ruined, and going downhill

A S SOON as my knees were sufficiently healed I was turned into a small meadow for a month or two. There was no one with me to keep me company, and I felt very lonely. Ginger and I had become fast friends and I missed her very much.

Then one morning the gate was opened, and who should come in but dear old Ginger. With a joyful whinny I trotted up to her. We were both glad to meet, but I soon found that it was not for our pleasure that she was put in the field with me. Her story would be too long to tell, but the end of it was that she had been ruined by hard riding, and was now put out to grass to see what rest would do.

We both knew that we were not the good horses we had been, but we did not let this spoil the joy we had in each other's company.

One day as we stood under the shady lime trees, we saw the Earl come into the meadow with York.

"There is three hundred pounds flung away," he said to York, looking closely at us. "But what I care about most is that my old friend entrusted me with these horses and now both are ruined. The mare shall have a year's grace, and we will see what rest will do for her. The black one must be sold, however. It is a great pity, but I cannot have a horse with knees like that in my stables."

"I know a man in Bath, my lord," said York, "the master of some livery stables, who often wants a good horse at a low figure."

"You had better write to him then," said his Lordship. "I'm more particular about the place and that he will be well cared for than the money he will fetch."

After this they left us.

About a week later, I was taken to the station, put in a horse box, and sent off on my journey. I cannot tell you how sad I was to say goodbye to Ginger or how sorry she was to see me go, but there was nothing we could do to alter the circumstances.

My new master kept a good many horses

and carriages of different kinds for hire.
And so it often happened that I was driven
by men who had no idea of how to treat a
horse. Some drivers gave me meaningless
cuts with the whip, while others drove with
such a tight rein that it became an agony
to walk or trot.

Once my driver took me over a road
where the stones were sharp and loose.
Soon a stone had lodged itself in one of my
forefeet. Furthermore, it was sharp on the
inside and round on the outside which, as
everyone knows, is the most dangerous
kind that a horse can pick up, for it cuts

his foot and at the same time makes him liable to stumble and fall.

My driver was laughing and talking to his passengers and for a while took no notice of my lameness. Realizing I was going a bit slower, he flapped his reins. Then he said, "Well, what do you know! They've sent me out with a lame horse! What a shame!"

Fortunately for me, a farmer on a stout cob came riding up to us. He stopped when he saw the trouble, got off his horse and gently picked up my foot. He tried hard to dislodge the stone, but it was now so tightly wedged that eventually he had to use a stone-pick.

"It's a wonder he didn't fall down and break his knees," the farmer said somewhat sternly. But my driver only laughed and said, "Why, he's just a hired horse, that's all."

Of course, sometimes we had good drivers. I remember one morning I was put into the light gig and taken to a house in Pulteney Street. Two gentlemen came out and the taller of them came round to my head and just shifted the collar with his hand to see if it fitted comfortably.

"I don't think this horse needs a curb," he said, patting my neck. "And I want it taken off."

Then he took the reins, and they both got up. I can remember even now how

quietly he turned me round, and then with a light feel of the rein, and a gentle touch of the whip across my back, we were off.

I arched my neck and set off at my best pace. I found I had someone behind me who knew how a good horse ought to be driven, and it seemed almost like old times again.

This gentleman took a great liking to me, and after trying me several times with the saddle, he persuaded my master to sell me to a friend of his who wanted a safe, pleasant horse for riding. And so it came to pass that in the summer I was sold to Mr Barry.

Who knows how long I might have stayed in my new home if it had not been for the grooms whom Mr Barry employed to look after me. The first, Filcher by name, was not only lazy and indifferent to my well-being, but also a thief. He stole the oats which my master bought to feed me.

In consequence, I grew so weak without the food I needed, that I could no longer carry my master at a fast pace.

Filcher's lazy, thieving ways were finally discovered and my kind-hearted master was suitably horrified at what had been going on. He sacked the groom and engaged another one, by name Alfred Smirk.

Smirk was a real humbug, having no care for my welfare in the least. But he saw to it that he was always brushing and patting me whenever my master came into the stable.

I had a loose box, and might have been comfortable if Smirk had not been too lazy to clean it out. He never took all the straw away and the smell and fumes from what lay underneath were so bad that it affected my eyes, and made me feel too ill to eat.

My master, of course, noticed the smell and questioned Smirk about it. He, however, just blamed it on the drains. A bricklayer was sent for immediately but, understandably, he found nothing amiss. Smirk continued to neglect me and my stable. When my master was busy, I often stood for days on end in the stable without stretching my legs at all.

"I don't know what is the matter with this horse," my master said often. "He is

so fumble-footed that I am afraid he will stumble and throw me." And one day this is just what happened. Mr Barry was not hurt and he wisely took me straight away to a farrier nearby.

"Your horse has got the 'thrush' and badly too," the farrier told him. "This is a complaint horses get if they stand too long in foul stables."

The next day I had my feet thoroughly cleaned and stuffed with tow soaked in some strong solution, and a very unpleasant business it was, too! The farrier ordered all the litter to be taken out of my box every day, and the floor to be kept very clean. Then I was to have bran mashes, a little green meat, and not as much corn as usual, till my feet were well again.

With this treatment I soon regained my spirits, but Mr Barry was so disgusted at being twice deceived by his grooms that he made up his mind to sell me as soon as I was sound again.

A London cab horse

NO DOUBT a horse fair is a very amusing place to those who have nothing to lose; at any rate there is plenty to see. At the one I recall now there were a good many horses in a similar condition to myself at that time, handsome and high-bred, but considered only middle class through some accident or blemish. There were others in their prime that were trotted out with a leading rein, the groom running at one side. But in the background there were a number of poor things, sadly broken down with hard work; their knees knuckling over, their hind legs swinging out at every step and their spirits long since broken.

I was put with two or three other strong, useful looking horses, and a good many people came to look at us. But the gentlemen always turned from me when they saw my broken knees.

There was one man who looked at me

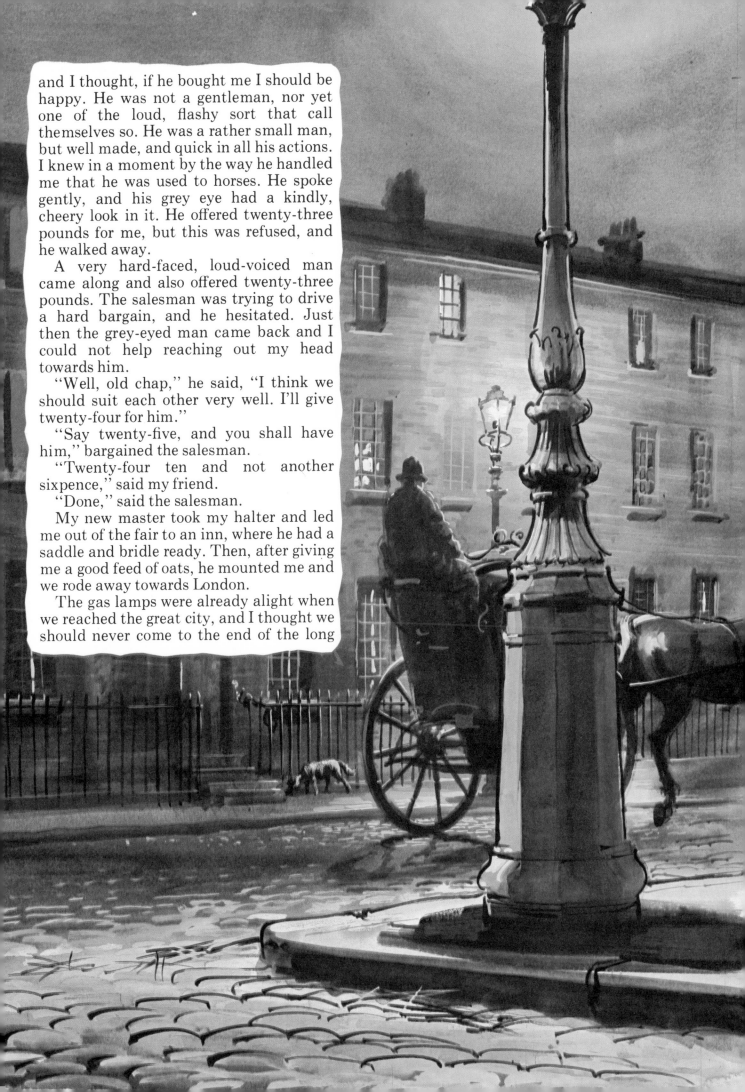

and I thought, if he bought me I should be happy. He was not a gentleman, nor yet one of the loud, flashy sort that call themselves so. He was a rather small man, but well made, and quick in all his actions. I knew in a moment by the way he handled me that he was used to horses. He spoke gently, and his grey eye had a kindly, cheery look in it. He offered twenty-three pounds for me, but this was refused, and he walked away.

A very hard-faced, loud-voiced man came along and also offered twenty-three pounds. The salesman was trying to drive a hard bargain, and he hesitated. Just then the grey-eyed man came back and I could not help reaching out my head towards him.

"Well, old chap," he said, "I think we should suit each other very well. I'll give twenty-four for him."

"Say twenty-five, and you shall have him," bargained the salesman.

"Twenty-four ten and not another sixpence," said my friend.

"Done," said the salesman.

My new master took my halter and led me out of the fair to an inn, where he had a saddle and bridle ready. Then, after giving me a good feed of oats, he mounted me and we rode away towards London.

The gas lamps were already alight when we reached the great city, and I thought we should never come to the end of the long streets that criss-crossed each other. However, we turned into one of the side streets at last and half way up that, into a very narrow street, with rather poor-looking houses on one side, and what seemed to be coach-houses and stables on the other.

My owner pulled up at one of the houses, and a kind-looking woman, followed by a little girl and boy, ran out. The next minute they were all standing round me in a small stable yard, and I felt the gentle pat of the little girl's hand on my neck.

My new master's name was Jeremiah Barker, but as everyone called him Jerry, I shall do the same. Polly, his wife, was a plump, tidy little woman, with smooth dark hair, dark eyes and a merry little mouth. Harry, the boy, was nearly twelve and Dolly was eight. They were all wonderfully fond of each other, and I never knew such a happy, merry family, before or since.

Jerry had a cab of his own, and two horses which he drove and attended to himself. His other horse was a tall, white, rather large-boned animal, called Captain, with a fine manner.

Having no way of knowing my name, Jerry called me Jack, and soon showed me that he would be the best of masters.

The next afternoon he took me out and drove me to a large cabstand. We pulled up in the rank at the back of the last cab, and almost at once the other cabmen came

to look me over. My new master seemed very content with me, especially when the oldest of the cabmen, Governor Grant, told him he had made a good buy.

The first week of my life as a cab horse was very trying. I had never been used to London, and the noise, the hurry, the crowds of horses, carts, and carriages that I had to make my way through, made me feel anxious and harassed. But I soon found that I could perfectly trust my driver, and I began to relax and get used to my new surroundings.

In a short time my master and I understood each other as well as horse and man can do. In the stable too, he did all that he could to make me and Captain comfortable, keeping us very clean and giving us plenty of good food. Not only that, we always had clean fresh water, night and day, except that is, of course, when we came in warm. But the best thing that we had was our rest-day on Sundays. Then Captain and I would stand enjoying each other's company and talking together about our former lives.

Jerry Barker

I NEVER KNEW a better man than my new master. He was kind and good, and as upright as John Manly. Harry, too, was a clever, gentle lad, and very good at helping in the stable. Polly and Dolly helped to make the cab neat and tidy each morning.

Jerry was dead against hard driving to please thoughtless people, though he always went a good fair pace. He was not against putting on the steam, as he put it, if he knew the reason for it.

I remember how once we took a young man to the South-Eastern Railway at a very fair pace indeed to save him from missing his train. I still had a very good mouth — that is, I could be guided by the slightest touch of the rein and, on that occasion, we got through the London traffic — carts, vans, trucks, cabs and great wagons — at a rapid trot.

We hurried into the station with just about eight minutes to spare to twelve o'clock — the time of the train.

"Thank God, we are in time," said the young man. "And thank you, my friend, and your good horse."

Then he tried to make Jerry accept an extra half-crown. But Jerry shook his head. "No, sir. Thank you all the same," was all he would say.

The other cabmen teased Jerry on his return when they discovered that he had refused the half-crown. But Jerry only smiled. He was happy that he had been able to do someone a service and he wanted no more than his dues.

Now although Jerry was set against Sunday work, there did come a Sunday when I was harnessed and taken out.

"Poor Dinah Brown's mother is very ill," Polly burst out, as she came into the stable on this particular Sunday morning when Jerry was feeding us. "She has only just heard and her mother's place is ten miles away, out in the country."

Jerry looked at me and then he nodded. "All right," he said, "I'll take her there."

It was a fine May day, and as soon as we were out of the town, the sweet air, and the smell of the fresh grass, began to make me feel quite young again.

When we reached the small farmhouse where Dinah's mother lived, my harness was taken off and I was left in the meadow. I did not know what to do first! Should I eat the grass, or roll over on my back, or lie down and rest, or have a gallop across the meadow out of sheer high spirits at being free? As it was I did all these things in turn, and how I enjoyed myself!

Jerry sat under a shady tree, singing to himself. Then he got up and picked some wild flowers and hawthorn for Polly.

It was a long time since I had had such a happy day, and when at last we went home again, I felt like a young colt!

Sad and happy days

ONE OF THE saddest days I remember was suddenly meeting Ginger again, pulling a shabby old cab. Poor Ginger, how changed she was! Her joints were grown out of shape with hard work and her face, once so handsome and full of spirit, was now full of suffering.

I was very much troubled and as we stood together I put my nose up to her.

Nothing I could say however could bring her comfort or relieve her from all her misery. A short time after our meeting, I saw a cart with a dead horse on it. It was a chestnut horse with a long, thin neck, and I believe it was Ginger. I hoped it was, for then her troubles would be over.

One of the few days in the year when Jerry could have as many fares as he could carry was Election Day. But he was so thoughtful that even on this day he would not overwork us. Indeed, he gave up some of the morning to taking a poor young woman, carrying a heavy child, to the hospital. And I shall never forget how warmly she thanked him, with tears in her eyes, as he helped her out of the cab.

On this day, the cabs with the candidates' colours on them were dashing about through the crowds and Jerry was not anxious to join in the throngs. Just as we left the hospital, however, a porter called "Cab!" We stopped, and a lady came down the steps. She seemed to recognize Jerry at once: "Barker, Jeremiah Barker!" she exclaimed. "Is it really you?"

"It is, ma'am," said Jerry. "And I'm glad to be able to serve you."

The lady asked to be taken to Paddington Station. We got there in good time for her train, and before leaving she enquired kindly after Polly, for, so I learnt, she was Polly's old mistress, Mrs Fowler. Then she said, "Now don't forget, Barker. Whenever you find this life too much for your health, let me know."

Strange to say, it was only a month or two after this meeting that Jerry caught a dreadful cold, which later turned into bronchitis. Harry took good care of us; and Governor Grant, the old cabman, was kind enough to give up the mornings to taking me out. On these occasions he handed over all that we earned to Polly.

One day, while Harry was in the stable, Dolly came in, full of excitement. "What do you think, Harry!" she cried. "Mrs Fowler has written to say we can all go and live near her. There is a cottage now empty that will suit us, and Father can take the place of her coachman who is leaving her. Country air will improve Father in no time at all."

"That's splendid!" said Harry, who was already trying to take on the burden of

supporting the family and was very worried about his father.

So it was quickly settled, and when Jerry was strong enough, they sold up everything and left London for ever.

We parted with deep sadness on both sides. The children were in tears and my generous-hearted master was deeply affected. He had sold me to a corn dealer and baker whom he knew, and with him he thought I should have good food and fair work.

A new life

MY NEW MASTER employed two
carters. My carter, whose name
was Jake, did his best to save me
from being overloaded, but the foreman
was a pushing, driving fellow with no con-
sideration for horses.

One day I was loaded more than usual,
and part of the road was on a steep incline.
I used all my strength, but I could not
climb it and was obliged continually to
stop. My driver laid the whip on badly,

again and again, and the pain of that great
cart whip was so sharp that I could
scarcely breathe. To be punished and
abused when I was doing my very best was
hard to understand and, in truth, it took
the heart out of me.

He was just raising the whip again when
a lady stepped quickly up to him and
begged him to stop flogging me. "Give him
his head altogether," she insisted in a
gentle earnest voice, "and see how much

better he will be able to pull that heavy load."

Jake agreed at last, and with the lady's encouragement I was able to reach the top of the hill. It was clear to the corn dealer, however, that I was not strong enough for his work, and so he sold me to a large cab owner.

I shall never forget my new master; he had black eyes and a hooked nose; his mouth was as full of teeth as a bulldog's, and his voice was as harsh as the grinding of cartwheels over gravel stones. His name was Nicholas Skinner.

Skinner had a low set of cabs and a low set of drivers, and the men were hard on the horses. We had no Sunday rest, and I joined their ranks in the heat of the summer.

I became so fevered and worn that I could hardly touch my food. My life was now so utterly wretched that I wished I might, like Ginger, drop down dead at my work. And one day my wish very nearly came to pass.

I went on the stand at eight in the morning and had done a good share of work, when we had to take a fare to the railway. There was a party of four, and a great deal of luggage.

The porter, who was attending to the heavy boxes, suggested to the driver that the load was too much for one cab. But the

driver laughed this aside, saying he could manage it all.

When at last the boxes were lodged on top of the cab, we drove out of the station. I was struggling to keep going, goaded on by the whip, but my feet slipped from under me and I fell heavily to the ground on my side. There I lay, the breath knocked out of my body, and I had neither power nor will to get up.

I heard someone say, "He's dead, he'll never rise again." Then cold water was thrown at my head. I cannot say how long I lay there, but at last, encouraged by a kind voice and a gentle hand, I staggered to my feet. Somebody led me quietly to some stables which were close by. I was put into a well-littered stall and given some warm gruel to drink.

In Skinner's eyes, I was now no good for anything but the slaughter house, but the farrier who attended me advised him to take good care of me for a few weeks and then send me to a horse fair just outside London. And to this he somewhat reluctantly agreed.

My last home

AT THIS sale I found myself in company with the old broken-down horses I mentioned before. The buyers and sellers looked not much better off than the poor beasts they were bargaining for.

Presently, coming from the better part of the fair, I noticed a man who looked like a gentleman farmer, with a young boy by his side. I saw his eyes rest on me, and I pricked up my ears and looked back at him.

"There's a horse, Willie," he said, "that has known better days."

"Poor old fellow," said the boy. "Do you think, Grandpapa, he was ever a carriage horse?"

"Indeed I do," said the farmer, coming closer.

I arched my poor, thin neck, raised my tail a little, and threw out my legs as well as I could for they were very stiff.

"What is the lowest you will take for him?" asked the farmer.

"Five pounds, sir," said the salesman.

"Very well," said Mr Thoroughgood, for that was his name, "I'll buy him."

After a good feed at the inn, I was gently ridden to my new home, and turned into a large meadow with a shed in one corner.

Willie was given charge of me, and he came every day with kind words and caresses.

The perfect rest, the good food and gentle exercise, soon began to tell on my condition and spirits. My legs improved and I began to feel fitter and younger again.

One day during the following summer, the groom cleaned and dressed me with such extraordinary care that I thought some new change must be at hand. Even the harness had an extra polish.

"If the ladies take to him," said the farmer to Willie, as they climbed into the chaise, "they'll be well suited and so will he."

A mile or two outside the village we stopped at a pretty, low house with a lawn and shrubbery at the front.

Willie rang the bell, and presently three ladies appeared. One was tall and pale, wrapped in a white shawl, and leaning on a younger lady, with dark eyes and a merry face. The third was tall and stately and my master addressed her as Miss Blomefield.

"I do not wish to influence you," said Mr Thoroughgood, as he patted my head. "But I think he is just the horse for you."

"Very well," said Miss Blomefield. "If my sister, Lavinia, sees no objection, we will accept your offer of a trial with thanks."

So it was arranged that I should be sent for the next day and, in the morning, a smart-looking man came for me. I was led away again, placed in a comfortable stable and fed. Then my groom began cleaning my face.

"That is just like the star that Black Beauty had," he said thoughtfully.

Then he began to look at me most carefully, all the while talking to himself.

"White star on the forehead, one white foot on the off side, a little knot in his neck where he was bled . . . . It *must* be Black Beauty. Why, Beauty, Beauty! Do you know me? Little Joe Green, that once almost killed you?" And he began patting and fondling me as if he was quite overjoyed.

I could not say that I remembered him, for now he was a fine-grown young fellow, with black whiskers and a man's voice.

But I was sure that he knew me and I put my nose up to him and tried to say that we were friends. I never saw a man so pleased.

"Well, well," he went on, "it won't be my fault, believe me, if you aren't well cared for now, for I shall do my very best for you. I wish John Manly was here to see you."

After this I was driven every day for a week or so, and as I appeared to be quite safe, my ladies decided to keep me. Joe had told them he was sure he knew me, and once again I was called Black Beauty.

I have now lived in this happy place a whole year. Joe is the best and kindest of grooms. My work is easy and pleasant and I feel my strength and spirits coming back all the time.

Willie always comes to see me when he visits the house and treats me as his special friend. My ladies have promised that I shall never be sold, and so I have nothing to fear. Here my story ends. My troubles are all over, and I am at peace. And sometimes, before I am quite awake, I fancy I am still in the orchard at Birtwick, standing with my old friends under the apple trees.